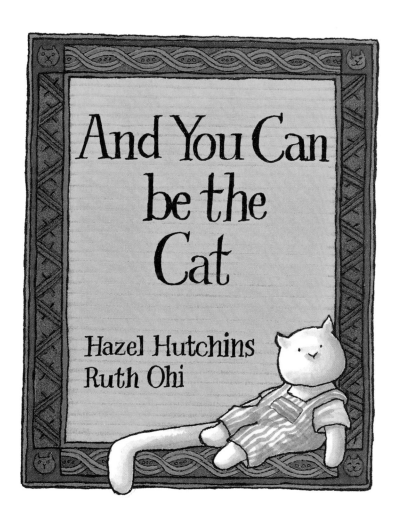

And You Can be the Cat

Hazel Hutchins
Ruth Ohi

Annick Press

© 1992 Hazel Hutchins (text)
© 1992 Ruth Ohi (art)
Designed by Ruth Ohi

Second printing, December 1992

Annick Press Ltd.

Annick Press gratefully acknowledges the support of the Canada
Council and the Ontario Arts Council.

Canadian Cataloguing in Publication Data

Hutchins, H.J. (Hazel J.)
    And you can be the cat

ISBN 1-55037-219-X (bound) ISBN 1-55037-216-5 (pbk.)

I. Ohi, Ruth. II. Title.

PS8565.U826A74 1992   jC813'.54   C91-905289-2
PZ7.H87An 1992

The art in this book was rendered in watercolour. The text has
been set in Goudy Oldstyle by Attic Typesetting.

Distributed in Canada by:
Firefly Books Ltd.
250 Sparks Avenue
Willowdale, Ontario   M2H 2S4

Distributed in the U.S.A. by:
Firefly Books (U.S.) Inc.
P.O. Box 1325
Ellicott Station
Buffalo, New York 14205

♾ Printed on acid-free paper.

Printed and bound in Canada by
D.W. Friesen and Sons, Altona, Manitoba

For Wil, Leanna and Ben

he day Neil came over wearing his fringed jacket and felt hat Leanna said to her little brother,—

"Norman, Neil and I are going to play pioneers. We are going to trek across the wilderness and build a cabin and plant crops. You are too little for most of this stuff but if you want to play you can be the cat."

"Meow," said Norman.

Norman liked being the pioneer cat. He rode on the back of the covered wagon and caught mice in the log cabin. He even helped the pioneer woman rescue the pioneer man from a pack of wolves.

The next day Neil came over again. He had a cash register beneath one arm and eighty-six thousand dollars in small bills tucked in his pockets.

"Norman," said Leanna. "Neil and I are going to play store. Neil is going to be the storekeeper and I'm going to be the delivery person and the customer. And you can be the cat."

"Meow," said Norman.

Norman liked being the store cat almost as much as being the pioneer cat—almost, but not quite. He caught mice in the back of the store and slept on a shelf in the front of the store and allowed the customer to pet him while Neil gave out the change. No, store cat was not as much fun as pioneer cat.

The next day Neil came over again. He was carrying a silver serving tray with a bow tie clamped on the side.

"Norman," said Leanna, "Neil and I are going to play fancy restaurant. I am going to be the waiter and Neil is going to be the customer and you can be the cat."

"I could be the cook," said Norman.

"The waiter cooks," said Leanna.

"I could be another customer," said Norman.

"Neil is going to change clothes every time and be all the customers we need," said Leanna.

"I could be—"

"The cat," said Leanna.

And she said it like she meant it.

So Norman was the cat. He was the kind of a cat that sat in the middle of the customer's table. He was the kind of a cat that howled when the customer tried to order from the menu. He was the kind of a cat that upset the spaghetti in the kitchen.

"This cat is not behaving," said Neil.

"Cats that do not behave have to live out in the alley," said Leanna.

And they sent Norman out into the hall and shut the door and barricaded it so he couldn't get back in.

orman was not a happy cat. He went into the living room to scratch the furniture. His father had washed the kitchen floor, and the kitchen chairs were all over the living room. Norman decided to build a fort where bossy waiters and mean customers could not find him.

He built a tower and wall and a drawbridge. He built a throne and a lookout post. He built a flagpole and a dungeon and a parapet (although he had no idea what a parapet was). When Neil and Leanna came out from the bedroom they were amazed at what they found.

"Norman, this is wonderful!" said Leanna.

"Norman, this is spectacular!" said Neil.

"Can we play too?" asked Leanna.

"Maybe," said Norman.

"We'll play castles and knights and dragons," said Leanna. "I will be the Royal Duchess who sings songs with her lute and tames fire-breathing dragons and does a bit of jousting on the side."

"And I will be the Duke who goes off looking for royal treasure and saving people from evil highwaymen and teaching knights how to knight and how not to knight," said Neil.

"And Norman, you can be the . . ." Leanna paused and looked at Norman.

Norman paused and looked at Leanna.

"You can be the King," finished Leanna. "You can be the King of the whole entire country who comes to inspect the castle and decree royal decrees and tell us about dragons that need taming and knights that need to be taught how to knight and how not to knight."

Norman smiled.

"No thanks," he said, pulling on his paddy paws and tucking his tail in the back of his pants. "I'll just be the cat."

And a very fine cat he was indeed.

D